The Doll's 1

By M.C. Leeka
Illustrated by County Studio

© 1993 McClanahan Book Company, Inc. All rights reserved.
Published by McClanahan Book Company, Inc.
23 West 26th Street, New York, NY 10010

Printed in the U.S.A.
ISBN 1-56293-343-4

In little Missy's bedroom
Shelves of toys adorned the wall.
And on a shelf beside her bed,
Was Missy's favorite doll.

Missy loved this special doll
Which she named Anne Marie.
And every afternoon at four,
She'd sit her down for tea.

At bedtime, Missy dressed the doll
In bedclothes like herself.
She'd give the doll a kiss goodnight,
Then put her on the shelf.

But then one quiet evening,
Something magical occurred.
As soon as Missy fell asleep,
Her doll began to stir.

In the darkness Anne Marie
Slipped out of her bedclothes.
She changed into a party dress
With fancy lace and bows.

Anne Marie climbed off her shelf
And down the bedroom wall.
She turned a light on and announced
"TEA TIME FOR ONE AND ALL!"

The teddy bear, the toy soldiers,
The lion and the clown,
All came alive in Missy's room
And started climbing down.

The toys were so excited
To be part of all the fun.
So Anne Marie got busy
Making tea for everyone.

The lion set the table and
The clown pulled up the chairs.
The toy soldiers were busy
Marching back and forth in pairs.

When everything was ready
Anne Marie called to her friends,
"Let's begin our tea party
Before the evening ends!"

She carried out the teapot
And a plate of cookies, too.
The teddy bear said, "Anne Marie,
I saved this seat for you!"

Anne Marie served all her guests
And then she took her seat.
She poured herself a cup of tea
And had a bite to eat.

Throughout the evening Missy slept,
Completely unaware
That Anne Marie was hosting
Such a fabulous affair.

Everybody ate and drank
Until the food was gone.
But then the party had to end
For it was nearing dawn.

A couple of toy soldiers
Quickly tidied up the scene.
The teddy bear and Anne Marie
Washed all the dishes clean.

Soon Missy's room was just as clean
As it had been before.
Every crumb of cookie had been
Picked up off the floor.

Everyone thanked Anne Marie
For having them to tea.
And then they climbed onto their shelves
And sat down quietly.

Anne Marie turned off the light
And climbed into her place.
She changed into her bedclothes
Then she wiped her hands and face.

When Missy woke that morning,
She was cheerful as could be.
She couldn't wait to start her day
And play with Anne Marie.

But then she noticed something
In the corner by the chair.
She took a closer look and saw
A teacup sitting there.

Missy picked the teacup up
And placed it on the shelf.
"Who could have left that teacup there?"
She wondered to herself.

"I'll think about the teacup
At another time," she said.
"Now let's get dressed!" she told her doll,
"There's so much fun ahead!"